THE
FLIMFLAM
MAN

THE
FLIMFLAM
MAN

Darleen Bailey Beard

Pictures by
Eileen Christelow

FARRAR STRAUS GIROUX
New York

Library of Congress Cataloging-in-Publication Data
Beard, Darleen Bailey.
    The flimflam man / Darleen Bailey Beard : pictures by Eileen
Christelow. —1st ed.
    p.   cm.
    Summary: In the summer of 1950, a con man comes to Wetumka,
Oklahoma, about his fabulous circus, and although he swindles the
townspeople, two young girls grow from the experience.
    ISBN 0-374-32346-1
    [1. Swindlers and swindling—Fiction.   2. Stuttering—Fiction.
3. Friendship—Fiction.   4. Oklahoma—Fiction.]   I. Christelow,
Eileen, ill.   II. Title.
PZ7.B374F1   1998   97-15606
[Fic]—DC21

Dedicated to the lovely people
of Wetumka, Oklahoma, who know how
to laugh with the best
of them

AUTHOR'S NOTE

This story is based on an incident which took place in the small farming town of Wetumka, Oklahoma, in July 1950, and which led to the Sucker Day Festival, celebrated by the town each August. To find out all about it, send a self-addressed, stamped business envelope to: Sucker Day Festival, Wetumka Chamber of Commerce, P.O. Box 275, Wetumka, Oklahoma 74883.

I would like to extend special thanks to the Wetumka residents who shared their memories of the event, including Jack and Jo Herring; PeeWee Nolen, also known as "Mr. Wetumka"; Orville Gammill; Elgie Absher; and Don Kardokus, city manager.

Special thanks also to Mindy Buie, speech therapist, and Pat VanDeventer, speech pathologist, who shared their expertise in language disorders, and to Wilmetta Miller, a dear friend and biographer of detail.

F. Bam Morrison is the name the flimflam man used when he came through Wetumka, and the character is based on the little we know about him. The other characters in this book are purely fictional.

THE
FLIMFLAM
MAN

1

It all started one scorching July day in 1950.

I'd been sitting in front of the Wide-A-Wake café since before the morning rush. The sun was burning my neck, and sweat dripped down my jumper, making it all wet and clammy, when along came mean Clara Jean. "Wh-Whatcha' g-got in th-the b-box, B-Bobbie Jo?" she asked, mimicking the way I talk.

"N-None of your beeswax," I said. Closing the flaps, I pulled the box toward me.

Clara Jean scrunched her lips. "You've got something in that box. Now, what is it?"

She stood there, hands on hips, wearing a long-sleeved blouse in the middle of July. She had on clear plastic rain boots, the kind that fit over shoes, only there were no shoes inside, just her dirty feet. I wanted to laugh but didn't dare.

"You better show me," Clara Jean insisted, stomping her foot.

I thought it over. If I didn't show her what was inside, she'd probably kick me. Or worse yet, kick the box. But if I *did* show her, she might move along and let me get on with my business. Slowly, I opened the flaps.

"Ohhh," she said, snatching up my brown-and-white puppy. "She's *sooo* cute. I'm taking her home with me right now."

"No!" I put my hands around the puppy and pulled, but Clara Jean hung on to her and wouldn't let go.

Now, I didn't hanker to sitting in front of the Wide-A-Wake all morning long, with sweat dripping down my back, asking folks, "Excuse me, would you like a free puppy? She'll make a good watchdog and she ain't got fleas, neither." But I would've sat there the rest of July before handing Daisy's last puppy over to Clara Jean. Why, I wouldn't give her a wooden nickel.

"L-Let go!" I gave my puppy a tug.

Clara Jean tugged right back.

Afraid we'd yank that poor thing right in half, tugging the way we were, I let my end go.

"Your box says *Free Puppies*," Clara Jean insisted. "So that means I can have her."

"N-No you can't. Now give her back."

"Give me one good reason why."

I could think of a thousand good reasons. Like the time she put sand in my sandwich. The time she yanked the poodle off my poodle skirt and slid it under the boys' bathroom door. And the time she laughed out loud when Mrs. Hampton asked me to stand and spell "opportunity."

But the only reason that came out of my mouth was a lie. A downright lie. And it slipped out quick as a wink. "B-Because she's already taken."

"If she's already taken, then why are you still sitting here?" She held the puppy on her head. "Do you like my new hair band?"

I wanted to punch her right in the face. But I couldn't. She was lots bigger than me. Eleven and a half. Eighteen months older. And mean as all get-out.

"I'm waiting for her new owner to come b-back and get her," I said, biting my lip.

"What new owner?"

I peered inside the Wide-A-Wake, but the breakfast crowd had already scattered.

I looked up and down Main Street. No one in sight.

Then I saw him—a fabulous fat man with a checkered vest, a gold pocket watch, and black-rimmed glasses, getting out of a turquoise Chevy. He wasn't anybody I'd ever seen before, which was pretty unusual in a town the size of Wetumka.

"Him," I said.

Clara Jean turned to see, and I stole my puppy right off her head before she could grab it back.

"Here's your fr-free puppy, mister," I said, shoving my puppy under his arm.

The man looked at me kind of strange like, then at my box and at Clara Jean. Then he smiled a snaggle-toothed smile. "This is just the pup I've been waiting for, little lady."

"It is?" I glanced at Clara Jean, not sure which of us was more surprised.

"Allow me to introduce myself," he said, holding out his hand. "My name is F. Bam Morrison, advance man for Bohn's United Circus Shows. You've seen our circus, haven't you?"

"No," I said.

His eyes grew big as turnips. "Why, that's impossible. Everyone knows about Bohn's United Circus Shows! What's your name, little lady?"

"Clara Jean Knox," Clara Jean butted in.

"Bobbie J-Jo Hailey," I said.

"Girls, you're in for a treat. Bohn's United Circus Shows are the most exciting, most thrilling, most daring shows you'll ever see. And in a few short days we're coming to . . ." He scratched his chin, then looked up and down the street. "What's the name of this town?"

"Wetumka!" Clara Jean said.

"Ah, yes. Wetumka, Oklahoma." He pulled a cigar

8

from his vest. "And this lucky pup will be our circus dog."

I was so surprised I reckon Clara Jean could've knocked me over with a feather. "D-D-Daddy always said someone in our family was bound to be famous. B-Bet he never dreamed it'd be Daisy's puppy."

"It's the opportunity of a lifetime!" Mr. Morrison agreed.

That gave me a mean idea. "O-p-p-o-r-t-u-n-i-t-y," I spelled out loud to Clara Jean. I said each letter nice and clear. She didn't even *snicker*.

When the lunch crowd arrived, the Wide-A-Wake smelled like sizzling onion burgers, crispy french fries, and chocolate pudding pie.

The pie went round and round in a high glass case that twirled automatically. Each slice had meringue, thick as a cloud, with chocolate shavings and mint leaves sprinkled on top.

I dug into my pocket, hoping there'd be more change than I remembered, but I had only enough to buy my usual, an RC and a bag of peanuts.

I poked the peanuts, one at a time, inside the bottle. Each peanut I named after a person. If the peanut floated, it meant that person was going to heaven. If the peanut sank, well, then that person wasn't.

Gus, the cook, shook his head. "Don't you go naming one of them spooky peanuts after me!"

"Too late," I teased. "B-Better start praying."

All around me, excitement buzzed like a bee. Silverware clattered. People chattered. Gus called, "Order up!" And the bell above the door kept right on ringing as more and more folks pressed in.

"Did you hear?" they asked, their faces gleaming.

"A circus."

"Right here in Wetumka!"

In walked Mr. Morrison, and a hush fell over the crowd. With everyone staring, he jumped right up on two barstools and started running, only he wasn't going anywhere. The stools went to spinning, and the faster they spun, the faster he talked: "Elephants . . . tightrope walkers . . . clowns. Dancing bears . . . tigers . . . no frowns. Men who eat fire. I'm no liar. Why, it's the best circus you'll ever see!"

Then he jumped back down, sending the stools into one final spin. Holding up his hands, he stared into the crowd, the way Pastor Regan does when he gets to the end of his sermon. "It's a shame," he said. "A crying shame. Some of you may not get to see Bohn's United Circus Shows."

We all looked at one another, confused like.

"Why not?" Clara Jean asked. "Isn't that why you're here? To sell tickets?"

"I do have a *few* advance tickets," Mr. Morrison said, looking into his vest pocket. "But not enough for the thousands of people who'll want to come.

"Why, do you folks realize that when the *Wetumka Gazette* prints *Bohn's United Circus Shows* in big bold letters, this town will be packed? Packed to the brim, I tell you. And seating is limited, you know."

Then he headed for the door, shaking his head.

"Wait!" Gus shouted. "Shouldn't we get first dibs on tickets?"

Mr. Morrison rubbed his chin. "I guess you're right."

Everyone crowded around, but I just sat there sipping my RC with peanuts. No need for me to push and shove. The only thing left in my pocket was a hopscotch stone, and I didn't reckon he'd make a trade.

"Ain't you going to get one?" Clara Jean asked,

holding her ticket right in front of my eyes so I couldn't see anything else.

"How'd you buy that?" I asked.

"With my grocery money," Clara Jean said. "How else?"

I ducked out from under her ticket, halfway wishing I could grab it and run. "My m-mama will get me one."

"We'll just wait and see," Clara Jean said, grinning. "Everyone knows when your daddy died he left you and your mama poor as orphans. By the time she saves enough, the tickets will all be gone."

My cheeks felt hotter than Gus's grill. How dare Clara Jean say my daddy left us poor. At least my mama took care of me. No one could say Clara Jean's daddy took care of her.

And then I said it, the worst thing I could possibly have said. The truth. "Well, everybody knows your d-daddy is a down-and-out drunk!" Then I bit my lip and closed my eyes.

It was a good thing, too. She punched me smack

dab in the nose, wiped the blood off her ticket, then started for the door.

"Wait!" I said, grabbing her arm. "I'm sorry."

"Sorry for what?" she asked, her eyes glaring.

And for the first time in my life, I was true-blue sorry. Sorry Clara Jean never got invited to slumber parties. Sorry she was going into the fifth grade when she should've been in sixth. And sorry I didn't like her.

I stood outside the Wide-A-Wake, folding in the flaps on my *Free Puppies* box, ready to head home.

My nose had finally stopped bleeding, but blood was all over the front of my jumper. I was figuring how I'd explain this to Mama, when Mr. Morrison stepped outside, holding my puppy under his arm.

"Bobbie Jo?" he asked, lighting up a cigar. "Would you be so kind as to show me where the hotel is?"

"Sure," I said, but I didn't feel very sociable. My nose was throbbing. My head ached. Even worse, I knew I'd hurt Clara Jean more with one sentence than she'd hurt me with all five fingers.

"Why the sad face, little lady?" Mr. Morrison asked. Then he noticed my jumper. "What in blue blazes happened?"

"I-I said something I shouldn't have."

"Oh, I see," Mr. Morrison said. "Well, we all say things we sometimes regret. I'm sure you didn't mean to."

"B-B-But I did. I hurt Clara Jean on purpose, 'cause she said my mama and I are poor as orphans."

Mr. Morrison took a deep puff on his cigar, then pulled something from his checkered-vest pocket. "You know, I've been thinking. You gave me this free circus pup, right?"

"Uh-huh."

"Then it just stands to reason that I should give you something in return. How'd you like a couple of tickets to Bohn's United Circus Shows?"

Before I could blink an eye, Mr. Morrison placed two red tickets in my hand. Black capital letters said: ADMIT ONE—BOHN'S UNITED CIRCUS SHOWS.

"I-I don't know what to say," I said, all embarrassed. I ran my fingers along the perforated part of the tickets, then quickly tucked them into my pocket, being careful not to bend the corners.

As we crossed Main Street, Mr. Morrison tipped

17

his hat and greeted passersby as if he'd known them all his life. He didn't seem a bit afraid to talk to anyone. And his words came out smooth as glass.

"M-Mr. Morrison? You sure do talk fine." I bit my lip. "I'll *never* be able to talk like that. I sound like a br-broken record."

"Would you believe that when I was younger, people could barely understand a word I said?"

"Really?"

"I knew a professor who owned a reel-to-reel tape recorder. You know, one of those machines that record music and such? Well, she suggested I record radio announcers, then repeat what they said into the recorder and play it back to listen to myself.

"At first I sounded something awful, as if my mouth was full of mush. But I practiced over and over until I learned to say each consonant, each vowel, almost like those fellows on the radio."

"How long d-d-did it take?"

"About two years."

"Two *years*? Wasn't that an awful long time?"

"Yes and no."

I thought about that. Two years seemed like forever. I wanted to talk well *now*.

Mr. Morrison tipped his hat as we passed ol' man Swank, who'd been sitting in front of Jim Ed's barbershop every day like clockwork for as long as I could remember.

Ol' man Swank was such an ornery old coot folks didn't pay him much nevermind. He was always ranting and raving about one thing or another. Last week, it was gasoline going up two cents a gallon. This week, President Truman.

"You the circus fella?" ol' man Swank asked, looking up from his checkerboard.

Mr. Morrison took a bow. "F. Bam Morrison, advance man for Bohn's United Circus Shows."

Ol' man Swank spat tobacco juice into a green-bean can and pointed a bony finger. "Bohn's United Circus, you say?"

"Finest show on earth."

Ol' man Swank raised an eyebrow and started waving his finger around.

"W-We best be going," I interrupted, knowing

that when ol' man Swank started waving his index finger, his ranting and raving was sure to follow.

Ol' man Swank harrumphed, then went back to playing checkers all by himself.

"Here we are," I said, stopping at Meadors Hotel. "Thanks for the free t-tickets."

"Thanks for the pup," he said. Then he looked real thoughtful, wiping perspiration off his forehead. "You don't happen to know anyone who'd want to hang up circus posters tomorrow morning, do you?"

"Me!"

"Good. Let's meet at the Wide-A-Wake café. Seven o'clock sharp."

I did a lot of thinking on my way home that day. About how I'd hide Mama's ticket under her pillow and tell her if she was hot or cold until she found it. About how Daisy's puppy was going to be famous. And how Mr. Morrison learned to talk like those radio announcers.

But most of all, I thought about how my daddy had left us a reel-to-reel tape recorder.

"Warmer . . . warmer . . . *hot!*"

Mama stood by her bed, looking at me as if I'd gone bananas. "Where? Where?" she squealed.

"You're burning hot!" I shouted. "You're on fire!"

Mama threw back the covers. She looked under the sheet. Under the bed.

"Colder. Colder."

She lifted up her pillow, and we both screamed at the sight of our tickets.

After supper, Mama made me change my jumper and we sat outside, drinking iced tea on our new screened-in porch. The porch wasn't new, just the screen part. We'd done it ourselves to help cut down on all the flies coming through the door. But so far, we couldn't tell much difference.

"So that Clara Jean just cold-cocked you, right in

22

the nose, for no reason?" Mama asked, looking up over her newspaper to make sure I was holding the ice bag the way she'd shown me.

"S-Sort of," I said, switching hands. The ice was cold.

Mama put down her paper and gave me her I-better-be-telling-the-truth look.

"She said that Daddy left us poor as orphans," I mumbled. And even softer, I said, "So I said her daddy is a down-and-out drunk."

"You didn't," Mama said.

I nodded. "But as soon as I said it, I was real sorry."

"Did you tell her?"

"Yes."

Mama scooted over on our porch swing and put her arm around me.

"M-Mama?" I bit my lip. "Are we poor?"

"Only in money. Not in spirit."

I thought about that, and I knew what she meant. "Clara Jean's daddy is poor in spirit, isn't he?"

Mama nodded. "He's been drinking as long as I've known him, and that's a mighty long time."

"Why doesn't he buy Clara Jean a pair of shoes?" I asked, nudging Daisy to move over.

"Reckon he spends all his money on other things. Drinking, mostly," Mama said. "If Clara Jean's mama knew her daughter was going around with no shoes, she'd roll over in her grave."

"How'd her mama die?"

"Car accident. Happened when Clara Jean was still a baby. Reckon that's why Clara Jean's daddy took to drinking."

I looked down at the wooden floor of our porch and pushed the swing with my big toe. "A-Are *you* going to start drinking?" My daddy had been gone three years.

"Heavens, no!" Mama squeezed me tight. "Drinking only adds problems. It doesn't solve them." She looked long and hard at my nose. "It's turning black and blue. I swear, if that Clara Jean was my daughter, I'd have horsewhipped her long ago."

25

I smiled, knowing Mama better. Why, she wouldn't horsewhip a horse, much less Clara Jean. Though I reckoned if she got ahold of Clara Jean's daddy, she might give it a try.

Only after Mama was sound asleep and snoring, and Daisy was all curled up in her dog box, did I dare to pull out the reel-to-reel tape recorder from under my bed. Mama had thought to sell it once, but I convinced her that daddy would have wanted us to keep it.

I turned on my radio, real low, and fiddled with the stations. "This is Wild Man Dan," a bouncy voice said, "and here's the new hit single that's rocking the charts."

I checked to make sure the old tape was working, then tried to say everything just as the voice had. But when I rewound the recorder and played it back, I sounded awful. Terrible. I tried a different channel.

"Another hot d-day in Oklahoma, with temperatures rising to one hundred d-degrees. Tomorrow's forecast coming up, after a brief m-message from Ivory, the soap so light it floats. And Frigidaire, the all-porcelain automatic washer. It washes, r-rinses, and spin-dries without your even being there. You can't m-match a Frigidaire!"

I stopped the recorder and shoved it under my bed. Why did I sound like a broken record? Nobody else going into fifth grade sounded like that. It just wasn't fair.

I stared at Daddy's picture, trying to hold it right so his eyes would look into mine. That wasn't fair, either. Why did Daddy's heart have to stop?

I opened the folded Chinese fan with roses on it that Mama bought me at the State Fair in Oklahoma City last summer, wondering what it'd be like to have an electric window unit. The man at the fair had one, and when I stood in front of it, it was like standing in front of the refrigerator. Nice cool air hit my face. He said everyone was buying them, even poor folks, but Mama shook her head, saying electric window units were for rich folks.

I turned off my radio, then stood at the window watching stars, the way Daddy and I used to. Daddy always said, "The sky's so pretty, the good Lord gift-wrapped it just for us."

But the sky wasn't near as pretty without him.

"There's my assistant!" Mr. Morrison shouted as I opened the door to the Wide-A-Wake.

The bell jingled above my head, and a waft of fresh-brewed coffee and crispy bacon hit my face. Gus's grill sizzled. Spoons tinkled in cups. Newspapers rustled. And folks chatted in low mumbles as I walked over to Mr. Morrison's table.

"Have a seat," Mr. Morrison said. "Breakfast is on me, little lady."

He handed me a menu, and I wasn't sure what to say. No one had ever bought me breakfast before.

"Go ahead and order," Mr. Morrison insisted. "I'm giving Gus free circus tickets in exchange for my meals. He won't mind if you order something."

"Orange juice and bacon, please."

"I'll have four eggs sunny-side up, two bowls of

29

grits, biscuits and gravy, and coffee," Mr. Morrison said. "And throw in a slice of apple pie for good measure."

I fingered my hopscotch stone and the red circus ticket with black capital letters in the pocket of my pedal pushers. "Mama s-says to tell you thanks for our t-t-tickets."

"You tell her she's as welcome as sunshine. And be sure to thank her for that terrific circus pup. They don't make pups like that every day, you know." He took a long, loud sip of his coffee.

"Wh-What are you going to name her?" I asked, fidgeting with the salt and pepper shakers.

Mr. Morrison looked up at the ceiling. "I've been thinking about Milly. Milly the Magnificent. It has a nice ring to it, don't you think?"

"Oh, yes!" My heart raced just hearing it. Milly the Magnificent! I couldn't wait to tell Mama and Daisy.

When Gus brought out our order, Mr. Morrison stuffed an entire biscuit right into his mouth, then washed it down with coffee. Gus's eyes grew big as walnuts.

The bell above the door kept right on ringing as more and more people scurried in, buzzing about Bohn's United Circus and that fabulous fat man, Mr. Morrison. "Do you have any tickets left?" they begged.

"Why, certainly," Mr. Morrison said. "But not for long. They're selling like hot cakes. Hey, that sounds pretty good." He called out to Gus, "Order of hot cakes, please!"

I didn't think I could watch him eat another bite, so I finished my orange juice and stood up real quick. "I b-better get an early start hanging up the p-posters."

"Put them in every window you can find," Mr. Morrison said, with egg yolk running down his chin. "Every wall, every fence, and anywhere else you can think of."

I put the posters in my bicycle basket and steered north on Main, figuring I'd work my way back south. But just as I was crossing Frisco, there came mean Clara Jean. She had on her usual plastic rain boots with a green Empire-waist dress that had a stain the size of Texas all across the front.

"Hi," I said, almost running right into her.

"Wh-What a s-surprise," Clara Jean mimicked, looking at my basket. "Wh-What are y-you d-doing?"

I gritted my teeth, forgetting how sorry I was for Clara Jean. How true-blue sorry I was. But then I remembered and forced a smile. "I'm hanging up posters. Want to help?" I hoped she had other plans.

"Sure," she said, her face lighting up like the town Christmas tree. Then her eyes looked real serious. "Sorry for making fun of the way you talk."

"Th-That's okay." Although it really wasn't. I hated when she did that.

"How's your nose? It looks kind of fat."

"It is," I said. "B-But I reckon it's my own fault."

"Sorry."

"D-Don't be. I shouldn't have bad-mouthed your daddy."

Clara Jean's eyes got all watery. She hung her head down and kicked my bicycle tire. "My daddy *is* a down-and-out drunk."

"No he's n-not," I stammered. I'd never seen Clara Jean cry. I didn't even know she could.

"It's true," she insisted. "Don't you think I know what people say about me and my daddy?"

I shook my head. *I* knew what they said, but I never dreamed *she* knew.

"They say, 'Don't look now, but there he goes. I saw his name in yesterday's paper. Arrested for disturbing the peace, you know.' And then they nod at me and say, 'Would you look at that poor pitiful girl? She'll never amount to anything. See the way she dresses? Ain't even got a decent pair of shoes.' Then they whisper and point. And I point right back."

I just stood there, holding up my bicycle, trying to think of something to say. But no words came.

"I'll show them," Clara Jean said, wiping her nose on her collar. "I'll show everyone. When I turn eighteen, I'm leaving this town and *never* coming back!"

"Where will you go?"

"Somewhere. Anywhere." Clara Jean sobbed. "As long as it's far from here."

Then something happened I couldn't quite explain. Right there on the corner of Main and Frisco, with folks passing and pickups rattling and dogs barking, I hugged mean Clara Jean, clear plastic rain boots, dirty feet, and all.

The sun was already scorching the sidewalks as Clara Jean and I worked our way up Main, hanging posters. When we reached Jim Ed's barbershop, there like clockwork sat ol' man Swank.

"Hi," I said, taking a rest on his bench.

He looked up from his checkers. "Whatcha got there?"

"P-Posters for the circus. Clara Jean and I are hanging them up all over town."

Ol' man Swank jumped three black checkers and crowned a red king. "You're wasting your time," he said, waving his bony finger. "Won't be no circus."

"B-But Mr. Morrison—"

"That rascal's nothin' but a flimflam man. All that fancy talkin' and hat-tippin' and hand-shakin' doesn't mean a dern fool thing. Have you seen any circus animals?"

"No. B-But—"

"Have you seen one single circus tent?"

"No," Clara Jean said, scooting in between us.

"Have you ever heard of Bohn's United Circus Shows?"

"Well, no. But—"

"Mark my words. That Mr. Morrison is a two-faced weasel. A traveling salesman, promising goods he can't deliver." He turned his checkerboard around to play the other side.

"That's not true," I finally got to say. "I'm h-his assistant. He even bought me breakfast—"

"On credit, no doubt." He slapped his knee and spat tobacco juice into his green-bean can. "That rascal's rooming at Meadors Hotel and boarding at the Wide-A-Wake, all in exchange for free tickets. He's even conned Doc Payne into a free checkup in exchange for an Indian blanket with fringe the doc will never see. Well, I'll tell you this—those tickets aren't worth the paper they're printed on . . ."

Ol' man Swank went right on ranting and raving, but I was too angry to listen. How could he say such awful things about Mr. Morrison? Mr. Morrison who talked as smooth as glass. Who made me his assistant. Who was going to turn Daisy's puppy into Milly the Magnificent.

". . . I didn't get to be ninety-six years old on my good looks alone. It took smarts. And plenty of 'em." He closed one eye. "In all my born days, I ain't never heard of Bohn's United Circus Shows."

Hearing ol' man Swank bad-mouth Mr. Morrison made me feel as if I'd swallowed Daisy's dog dish. And it wasn't very tasty.

"My daddy says ol' man Swank is crotchety," Clara Jean said when we finally got down the street.

I wasn't right sure what *crotchety* meant and was too proud to ask, but just the way it sounded made me smile.

"Daddy says you can't believe a word he tells you. He says ol' man Swank is full of beans!"

"But what if ol' man Swank is right? What if Mr. Morrison's t-tickets aren't worth the paper they're pr-printed on?" I took the red ticket out of my pocket and inspected it carefully: ADMIT ONE—BOHN'S UNITED CIRCUS SHOWS.

"Let me see." Clara Jean swiped it right out of my hand. "Did your mama buy this?"

"Mr. Morrison g-gave it to me in exchange for Milly the Magnificent."

"Milly the who?"

"Milly the Magnificent. Th-That's what he's naming Daisy's puppy."

"There. You see?" Clara Jean said. "Mr. Morrison wouldn't name your puppy Milly the Magnificent if he didn't have a circus. Now, would he?"

"I reckon not."

"Then that's proof enough," Clara Jean said, giving me back my ticket.

Just as we were taping our last poster in the front window of Meadors Hotel, out stepped Mr. Morrison. He was all gussied up in a gold sequined vest and boots made out of some kind of skin I'd never seen.

"How's my assistant?" he asked, standing back to admire his reflection in the window.

"F-Fine," I said. But it wasn't true. Seeing him made my insides queasy.

Clara Jean nudged me with her elbow.

I nudged her back.

She nudged me again, pushing me right into Mr. Morrison, whispering real loud, "You ask him."

"Ask me what?" Mr. Morrison said. He pulled out a cigar and struck a match on his boot.

I bit my lip. I didn't want to ask him, but since I'd been elected, I gave it my best shot. "Wh-Where's the circus animals?"

"They're coming," he said. "The tigers and bears should be here tomorrow, but the elephants take a little longer, being so heavy and all."

"You see?" Clara Jean butted in. "Ol' man Swank was wrong. Mr. Morrison is telling the truth."

"Did someone say I wasn't?"

"Ol' man Swank said you're a flimflam man," Clara Jean said. "A rascal. And something called a two-faced weasel. What's a two-faced weasel?"

I elbowed Clara Jean and yanked on the back of her ugly green dress. How dare she tell Mr. Morrison all those awful things.

"A two-faced weasel is someone who shows one face in public but hides another face for his evil deeds," Mr. Morrison said. He turned around and parted his hair. "Do you see another face back there?"

Clara Jean and I giggled and shook our heads.

I bit my lip again. "Y-You promise the animals are coming?"

He held up two fingers. "Scout's honor." And off he headed across the brick street, tipping his hat to the women of the Good Ladies Society, who were planting marigolds in front of the Bank of Commerce.

"That's the spirit!" Mr. Morrison cheered. "Bohn's United Circus Shows will do your town proud. Plant flowers. Wash windows. Wave flags from every doorway. Oh, by the way, could you plant a few of those flowers in front of Meadors Hotel? It could use a little sprucing up. And Doc Payne's office could use a friendly coat of paint on his sign out front."

The ladies looked at each other, smiling and wiping their foreheads. "We'd be delighted. Anything to help you."

Mr. Morrison bowed, then went on down the street.

"Wait!" Clara Jean shouted, running after him.

The hem of her dress was ripped and hung down kind of low. "Where are you going?"

"Sh-She means, are there any more posters to hang?" I didn't want Mr. Morrison to think his assistant ran around with an odd duck. Though no duck could be much odder than Clara Jean.

Mr. Morrison thought for a minute, leaning against the flagpole that stood right in the middle of Main and Broadway. "How would you two like to come along and help sell advertising for the circus program?"

"Swell!" Clara Jean said.

"S-Sure," I said. And I rode my bike between them.

Mrs. Clark was sweeping her floor as the three of us came up to the door of Murphy's Cleaners. Just as Mr. Morrison was about to step inside, a batch of dirt flew right out the doorway and landed on his fancy boots.

"Oh, I'm so sorry!" Mrs. Clark said, trying to sweep the dirt off. She quickly pushed back loose strands of hair and wiped her hands on her apron. "Mr. Morrison? How nice to see you."

Mr. Morrison stomped his boots, then did something I'd never seen before. At least not in real life. I'd seen it once through the window of Herring's Hardware, on a television show. In broad daylight, he picked up Mrs. Clark's hand and kissed it, right on top.

Mrs. Clark glanced at me and Clara Jean. Then

her cheeks turned as red as the tomato on our kitchen windowsill. "How can I help you, Mr. Morrison?"

"It's not how *you* can help *me*," he said, still holding her hand. "It's how *I* can help *you*."

Taking back her hand, she finger-combed more loose strands of hair and smoothed her apron. "Please, come in out of the sun," she said.

Clara Jean and I took a seat nice and quiet, but I was about to burst out laughing. I never heard anybody talk smoother than that Mr. Morrison. And Clara Jean mustn't have either, 'cause her mouth dropped clear open. A fly could've flown in and roasted marshmallows and she wouldn't even have noticed.

"As you know, Bohn's United Circus Shows will be arriving in its entirety in a few short days," Mr. Morrison said. "I thought I'd give you the first opportunity to advertise in our circus program. You do want thousands of circus-goers to see 'Murphy's Cleaners' in big bold letters on the front page, don't you?"

"Why, yes." She went over to her money tin and took out some change. "Will this be enough?"

Mr. Morrison rubbed his chin. "Enough for a teeny tiny ad. But you want big. You want bold. You want everyone to know 'Murphy's Cleaners Removes Tough Stains, Even Gravy.' You *can* remove gravy stains, can't you?"

"I certainly can." She looked real determined and dug into her apron pocket. "How's this?"

"Better," Mr. Morrison said. "But can you remove beet juice? How about those nasty blueberry-pie stains?"

"Yes, yes! I can remove all of those!"

"Then you'll need a big ad," Mr. Morrison insisted. "That'll be a dollar more."

Mrs. Clark went into her back room and came out with a dollar.

"Perfect!" Mr. Morrison gave her hand another kiss. "Now write your advertisement. Be sure to mention the blueberry-pie stains. And my assistant will pick it up tomorrow."

I smiled politely and stood up real straight like, so she'd know I was the assistant, not Clara Jean. Clara Jean elbowed me when I sat back down.

The rest of the afternoon, the three of us went around selling advertisements to almost every shop in town—the Redskin Theater, the Wide-A-Wake café, the Farmers Exchange, the Bank of Commerce, Herring's Hardware, and T. P. Mercantile.

"I can see it now," Mr. Morrison told Pastor Regan. "Your church's name—in big, bold letters. Why, the pews will be so chock-full of sinners, you'll have to give *two* altar calls."

"Hallelujah!" shouted Pastor Regan. And he handed Mr. Morrison some cash.

Mr. Morrison tucked the cash in his pocket, then whispered real confidential like, "Did I mention that Pastor Gann's church across the street is advertising, too? I heard tell their men's softball team beat yours two years in a row."

"Oh, you did, did you?" Pastor Regan's nostrils flared. He dug down into his pocket and came up with another dollar, a quarter, and three pennies. "You tell Gann we'll take on his boys anytime anywhere."

"I'll do that," Mr. Morrison said, shaking Pastor Regan's hand. "God bless you."

By midafternoon, the back of my blouse was as damp as a mop. Clara Jean was fanning herself with a sycamore leaf, and Mr. Morrison was all red-faced, with round, wet marks in the armpits of his shirt.

We stopped in at Gammill's gasoline station and got three ice-cold RCs and two bags of peanuts from the machines, in exchange for free circus tickets. While Mr. Morrison went inside and gave his sales pitch, Clara Jean and I found a nice shady spot outside.

I named my first peanut Mr. Morrison, then poked it in my bottle. It sank clear to the bottom. I poked in another; it sank, too.

Clara Jean put a peanut in her bottle, then gasped.

I covered her mouth. "It's just a game. A s-silly old game that d-doesn't mean a thing."

"You're right," Clara Jean said. "It's a stupid game. We shouldn't even bother to play it." And she poured all her peanuts into her bottle and shook it up. The peanuts swirled like a tiny tornado, and we drank our RCs without another word.

By the time Mr. Morrison stepped out of Gammill's, Clara Jean and I had finished our drinks and eaten most of our peanuts. Some of the peanuts stuck to the bottom of the bottles. But we were used to that.

"That about wraps it up!" Mr. Morrison said, patting his vest pocket, where he kept all his money.

"How much money have you gotten so far?" Clara Jean asked.

I elbowed Clara Jean and gave her a mean look. Mr. Morrison must have thought she had no manners at all.

Mr. Morrison took out his billfold and started thumbing through it. He lit up a cigar. "Let's see, now." He counted and did some figuring, then grinned his snaggle-toothed grin. "Looks like I've got about two hundred and fifty dollars."

I almost fell off my bicycle. Two hundred and fifty dollars! That was more money than Pastor Regan collected in a whole month of Sundays. Why, I'd never seen that much money in all my life!

"Can I hold it?" Clara Jean asked, almost walking right into me. "I ain't never held that much money."

"Be real careful," Mr. Morrison said. He handed her the money and Clara Jean just stood there, fists full of dollars, smiling as if she'd died and gone to heaven.

I wanted to hold the money, too. But I couldn't bring myself to ask. I just kept on ride-walking real slow, wondering what it'd be like to have all that money.

Why, if I had that money, I'd buy me and Mama one of those electric window units that blew cold air right on our faces. I'd buy us a television set so we could watch in our own home and not have to stand in front of Herring's Hardware, pushing and shoving to see. And I'd get my daddy one of those

fancy marble tombstones with weeping angels and scrolls.

Clara Jean must have been thinking about all the stuff she'd buy, 'cause her eyes had a faraway look. Then she glanced down at her clear plastic rain boots and handed back the money, looking right sad.

I looked down at my saddle oxfords and felt sinful. Just plumb evil. There I was, buying fancy electric window units, television sets, and marble tombstones, when Clara Jean was probably buying shoes. Plain ol' shoes.

I swore right then that if I ever got some money I'd buy Clara Jean a pair of shoes. Fancy shoes, like movie stars wear. With high heels and diamond buckles.

As we neared the Wide-A-Wake, the smell of onion burgers and strawberry malts reminded me that it was suppertime.

Mama didn't take to me being late for supper, especially on meat-loaf night. That was when she set out our plates that didn't have chips and poured iced tea in the wineglasses from her and Daddy's wedding.

"I'd b-best be going," I said, turning my bicycle in the direction of home. "D-Do you want us to help out tomorrow?"

Mr. Morrison rubbed his chin and struck another match on his boot.

"There's lots more we can do," Clara Jean butted in. "Like collect everyone's advertisements. Help put up the circus tent. Gather hay for the elephants. And oats for—"

"Meet me in front of the Wide-A-Wake café," Mr. Morrison said. "Seven o'clock sharp."

"Yes, sir!" Clara Jean took off, real excited like.

"Little lady?" Mr. Morrison said, lighting up his cigar.

"Yes?"

"You remember, now, what I told you about the reel-to-reel tape recorder?"

"Uh-huh."

"And remember, some things don't work out the

way you want them to. But they always work out in the end."

"Okay," I said, and when I turned to look back, he'd disappeared into the Wide-A-Wake.

10

After supper that night, Mama and I did the usual. I washed. She dried, making sure to put up the wineglasses first thing, so they wouldn't break.

I did most of the talking and she did most of the uh-humming. I told her about all the money Mr. Morrison had made, how Clara Jean got to hold it but I was too embarrassed to ask. About Milly the Magnificent. And the funny way Pastor Regan's nostrils flared when Mr. Morrison mentioned our softball team's losing streak.

"Speaking about Pastor Regan," Mama said, clearing her throat. "I've invited him over for supper next Wednesday night."

I almost dropped our iced-tea pitcher. "You mean here? To eat? J-Just like that?"

"Yes."

The last time Pastor Regan came over was when Daddy died. And the time before that, when Daddy was sick. "Mama?" I bit my lip. "Are you sick?"

"Not at all," Mama said. Dropping the meatloaf pan in my dishwater, she gave me a hug. "I just thought it was high time to have the pastor over for a *good* reason, instead of a sad one. That's all."

I scrubbed the pan real hard, trying to get the crusty parts, thinking about what Mama had said.

"But what about Daddy's chair?"

"What about it?"

"Will Pastor Regan sit in it?" I couldn't bear to look at Mama's face.

"Of course not," Mama said. She lifted my chin. "He's only coming for supper. Not to take Daddy's place."

I swished the dishwater with my scrubber.

"I thought we'd have supper outside on our new screened-in porch. I'll borrow a folding table and cover it with our white tablecloth. We can even buy some of those cream puffs you like so well from the bakery."

White tablecloth? Cream puffs? Mama didn't go to all that trouble for just anybody. My stomach felt kind of funny.

After we wiped down the stove and fed Daisy, Mama and I walked from room to room, shooing flies with a tea towel. I held one corner, she held the other. Then we snuck up, real quiet, and herded them out of each room. When we got to the kitchen, I pushed open the screen door while Mama shooed them out.

Mama tried to make like it was fun shooing flies. But I knew better. She didn't like it any more than I did. That was why she was always saving cotton out of our aspirin bottles and sticking little pieces in the holes on our screens.

Mama said the flies would think the cotton was spider eggs. Then they'd stay away for fear of getting trapped in a spiderweb. But our flies must've caught on to her plan, 'cause we still had to shoo them out once a day. Twice, when company came.

Mama was like that. Always trying to make things seem fun, even if they weren't. That was why I didn't want her to know about me practicing on the reel-to-reel tape recorder. That was no fun at all. It was plain hard work. So I kept my practicing all to myself.

"T-Temperatures zoomed to one hundred and two degrees today," I repeated, trying to say each word nice and smooth. "Cooler weather is pre-predicted for tomorrow with a high of ninety degrees. T-Today's weather is brought to you by the six flavors of Kool-Aid. One package makes ten big, cold drinks."

I rewound the recorder and listened. I sounded awful.

Why did I talk like a baby? In two years, I'd be twelve—I might even need a bra. Oh, why wasn't my voice cooperating?

I glanced over at Daddy's picture. His eyes were

looking right at me. I got a funny feeling that he knew what I was doing. That he planned it this way.

Daisy and I looked out the window. "I'll practice talking for you, Daddy," I said softly. "You'll see. And don't you worry about Pastor Regan. I'll make sure he doesn't sit in your chair."

11

Ten minutes after seven, I stood with my bicycle outside the Wide-A-Wake. I was a little late because Daisy followed me and I had to chase her back home and close our gate.

The breakfast crowd had mostly gone, but a few farmers sat inside, sipping coffee and reading the *Wetumka Gazette.*

I looked around but didn't see Clara Jean or Mr. Morrison. Surely they wouldn't leave without me.

"Guess who?" Clara Jean said, covering my eyes with her hands.

"I know who," I said, but her hands wouldn't budge.

"Guess."

"Okay," I said, feeling all over her hair and face. "Ummm . . . M-Mr. Morrison?"

"No, silly!" She thumped my head. "Where *is* Mr. Morrison?"

"H-He's not here yet."

Clara Jean was wearing her usual clear plastic rain boots, with no shoes inside. She had on another long-sleeved blouse with a couple of buttons missing and a skirt so worn it looked as if it belonged in Daisy's dog box.

After a while, we got tired of standing, so we sat on the curb and recited the Pledge of Allegiance. Eight times. We counted four cars, two trucks, and one flat-bed trailer.

We played three games of hopscotch, then took turns saying that the next boy who walked by would be the other one's husband. And when Mr. Morrison still didn't show up, we played Hang Man in the dirt with a stick.

"Mr. Morrison must've forgot," Clara Jean said, scraping her stick between the bricks in the street. "I don't think he's coming."

I opened the door to the Wide-A-Wake.

"Have y-you seen Mr. Morrison?" I asked Gus.

"Sure enough. Came in about six o'clock. That fella ate nine pancakes!"

Clara Jean gasped. I wasn't right sure if it was because she'd never heard of anybody eating nine pancakes, or if she was putting two and two together, same as I was.

"C-Come on," I told her. "Let's find him."

We hurried across Main Street to Meadors Hotel. "Have you seen Mr. Morrison?"

The clerk sighed real soft, then looked at the top of her hand. "After he kissed my—I mean, said goodbye, he headed toward the Wide-A-Wake early this morning."

My thoughts started racing. What if ol' man Swank was right? What if Mr. Morrison *was* a no-good flimflam man? A two-faced weasel.

I bit my lip. "D-Did he check out when he left?"

"No," she said. "But when I made his bed, I noticed all his clothes were gone. Even that darling puppy."

I stepped back outside and did some quick thinking. If anyone in town knew where Mr. Morrison was, it had to be ol' man Swank.

I bicycled past the Bank of Commerce, with Clara Jean running behind. Even before I reached Jim Ed's barbershop, I shouted, "H-Have you seen Mr. Morrison?"

Ol' man Swank nodded, chewing on a shiny new nail as if it were a toothpick.

"When?" Clara Jean asked.

"Reckon not more than ten minutes ago," he said, jumping a red checker.

"Which way did he go?"

"North." Ol' man Swank started waving his bony finger. "You mark my words. That rascal's heading out of town with everybody's money. But I made sure he'd have a hard time leavin'. Matter o' fact, he should be stoppin' right about now."

"Why?"

"You'll see," ol' man Swank said, spitting tobacco juice into his can. "That flimflam man can't pull the wool over this old geezer's eyes. Yes-siree, I've seen his kind come and go. Why, in my day . . ."

Clara Jean and I bolted northward, leaving ol' man Swank ranting and raving to nobody but himself.

12

I pedaled so fast Clara Jean must've thought I was training for the Olympics.

"Hey!" she shouted. "Wait up. Let me ride double-decker on your handlebars!"

I stopped to catch my breath. There was no way I could pedal Clara Jean on my bicycle. She was twice my size. Besides, Mama had told me never to let anyone ride double-decker. She knew someone who got killed that way.

"Here, y-you take my bicycle. I'll run."

Clara Jean took the handlebars. "You can't run fast enough. If we're going to catch him, *you* ride double-decker and *I'll* pedal."

Mama never told *me* not to ride double-decker, so without a second thought I hopped onto the handlebars and off we sped, bumping over the railroad tracks and past the water plant.

When Clara Jean and I pedaled by Harvey's gasoline station at the edge of town, my heart flip-flopped. There sat Milly the Magnificent, tied to the gas pump.

"Wh-Where's Mr. Morrison?" I cried.

"Don't know," Harvey said. "He left just a few minutes ago. Traded this here circus pup for a whole tank of gas. Said she could walk on her hind feet and balance a ball on her nose."

My heart did another flip-flop. I felt as if I'd swallowed Daisy's dog dish all over again. Only this time it was full of dirt.

"Which way did he go?" Clara Jean shouted.

"Yonder," Harvey said, pointing north over the oil field, "toward Highway 75."

I reckoned if Mr. Morrison got on the highway he'd be out of town in nothing flat. If we were going to beat him to the highway, we'd have to take the short cut through the oil field. The one with a sign posted: KEEP OUT.

Clara Jean and I didn't even discuss it. We just headed for the oil field, knowing it was the only way.

The dirt road was bumpy and dusty and full of ruts from the big tanker trucks that loaded up the oil. It was all I could do to hang on, and by the look on Clara Jean's red face, I knew it was all she could do to keep pedaling.

"D-Do you want me to get off and run?" I asked, half afraid we'd fall and half worried Mama'd find out.

"Hang on!" Clara Jean said. "Hang on!"

All that bouncing and bumping made my thoughts tumble out. How could Mr. Morrison do this? He'd given me Scout's honor. He'd promised.

And the more I thought about it, the angrier I got. Who did he think he was? Just waltzing into Wetumka as if he owned the place. I wanted to punch him right in the nose. I wanted to—

"Ohhh!" Clara Jean shouted. The bicycle started wobbling all over the road. "Look out!"

About ten feet away was a huge, pumping oil rig.

"Hit the brakes!" I screamed.

Then everything went black.

13

There were no sights, no sounds, only darkness.

Then I felt raindrops. Right on my cheeks.

I opened my eyes. Two Clara Jeans were looking down at me, crying.

"Oh, thank goodness!" she said, grabbing me and hugging my face. "I thought—I thought you were—"

"Dead?" I asked. My head felt as if it weighed a ton.

"Where a-am I?"

"We're in the oil field," Clara Jean said. "We just crashed your bicycle chasing after Mr. Morrison. Remember?"

"I remember," I said, trying to get up.

Clara Jean sighed and let go of my cheeks. "What a relief. For a minute I thought you had amnesia." Then she helped me to my feet, even though her skirt was stuck in the bicycle chain and she could barely move.

I tried to untangle her skirt, but the bicycle chain's teeth bit into it like an angry dog and wouldn't let go.

"It's no use," Clara Jean said, hunched over my bicycle. "You go on without me."

"But I can't just leave you—"

"Go!"

I took off running. And just as I turned the bend onto Highway 75, there sat Mr. Morrison's turquoise Chevy. But I didn't see him.

I ran around the side of his car and found him, head bent over, looking at a flat tire with a shiny new nail in it. That ol' man Swank didn't miss a trick. I would have laughed if I hadn't been so mad.

"You lied to me!" I shouted. "You gave me Scout's honor!"

"Sorry, little lady," Mr. Morrison said, kicking his tire.

" 'Sorry, little lady'? Is that all you have to say?"

"Look, Bobbie Jo, just because I didn't keep my promise doesn't mean I don't care about you."

"If y-you cared so much about me, you wouldn't have lied. You probably even lied about that reel-to-reel tape recorder, didn't you?"

"Yes. But—"

That dirty, rotten liar! I turned around, running, not wanting to hear another word. But he started his Chevy and drove up even with me so I'd have to hear him talk.

"I didn't have a speech problem when I was little," he said over the thumping of his flat tire. "But I read about a fellow who did. He really *did* talk into one of those recorders. And it helped him."

I didn't answer. Why should I allow myself to believe another word? He was a crook. A liar. A *three*-faced weasel.

"You've got to believe me. I never meant to hurt you."

"B-But you did!" I yelled right in his ear. "You hurt *me* and everyone else in Wetumka. We *believed* in you."

"I'm sorry," he said. "Sorry I lied to you. Sorry I don't have a circus. Sorry I can't stay."

And the look in his eyes was real. True-blue real. Like the sorry I felt for Clara Jean. Like the way I wished I could've taken back what I'd said about her daddy. And like the pain I felt right then, as Mr. Morrison thumped off down the road onto Highway 75.

I stood there, watching until his Chevy was a tiny turquoise speck. Smaller than the flies Mama and I shoo out our kitchen door.

14

"He's gone," I told Clara Jean, bursting into tears.

"I know." Clara Jean handed me a portion of her skirt. "Go ahead, blow your nose."

Her skirt had a big rip. All around, it was black and greasy, and she had smudges on her hands and cheeks.

"Our peanuts were right, you know," Clara Jean said. "We should've listened to them."

I sat down in the grass, staring into the oil field. The oil rigs pumped up and down, making their soft click-clicking sound, as if nothing had ever happened.

Clara Jean plopped next to me and we just sat there, as if in some kind of trance. Our hair blew hot and dusty, right in each other's eyes. But we didn't care a bit.

"I-I got this funny feeling he was really sorry. True-blue sorry. But like he thought it w-was too late to undo all the wrong he'd done. Or maybe h-he was just too plain embarrassed to face everyone."

Clara Jean's eyes got all watery. "I wonder if that's how my daddy feels? Do you think he'll ever change?"

I bit my lip. "Don't rightly know. But I reckon *y-you'll* change."

"Me? How?"

"The way you said. You'll move off somewhere. Get a job—"

"Teaching," Clara Jean said. "I want to be a schoolteacher, like Mrs. Hampton. And wear pink high heels like she wears. And on Sundays I'll wear white sandals with pearl buttons and paint my toenails watermelon red. And on Easter—"

I covered Clara Jean's mouth. "R-Right now, we need to come up with a plan."

"A plan? For what?"

"We can't just stroll back into town, telling every-one there's no cir-circus," I said. "They'll feel like fools!"

"Not ol' man Swank," Clara Jean said. "He'll feel proud as a peacock. Can't you just see him strutting around town, waving that bony finger of his?"

"And s-saying, 'Why, in all m-my born days, I ain't never heard of—' "

"Watch this." Clara Jean stood up, all hunched over like ol' man Swank. She closed her lips and put her tongue between her bottom lip and her teeth and started waving her index finger around.

Showering her with a handful of grass, I realized that I kind of envied Clara Jean. She wasn't a bit shy. She always spoke what was on her mind. And she did a swell impression of ol' man Swank.

"You sh-should be an actress," I said, tossing more grass her way.

"You really think so?" Clara Jean waved her finger at me and pretended to spit tobacco juice.

"Yes," I said. "You're a n-natural."

Clara Jean's face beamed. For a minute, I thought she might cry.

"So"—Clara Jean's voice cracked—"how *do* we tell everyone that there's not going to be a circus?"

For a minute, I didn't answer. I just sat there, watching the oil rigs click-click-clicking like giant seesaws. Every once in a while, one of them would backfire, sounding like a tremendous gunshot. But nothing seemed to disrupt them. And suddenly I said, "The show must go on."

"Are you crazy?" Clara Jean asked, knocking on the top of my head. "How can the show go on if there *is* no show?"

"Who says the show has to b-b-be a circus?" I asked. I walked over to my bicycle. The front wheel was cockeyed. I straightened it out and started riding real slow so Clara Jean could keep up.

"But if it's not a circus, what will it be?"

"A parade."

"I don't know . . ." Clara Jean said, wiping her hands and face on her skirt. "A parade's not much, compared to a circus."

"H-How about a parade with arts and crafts? And hot dogs. And lemonade."

"Well, maybe . . ."

"With a watermelon-seed-spitting contest," I said. "A-A pie-eating contest. A hay grab with one- and five-dollar bills. A hog-calling contest. And a-a—"

"Cow-chip-throwing contest!" Clara Jean said.

I stopped riding and looked at Clara Jean as if she'd grown antlers. "You wouldn't *really* pick up a cow chip, would you?"

"Sure. I've picked them up plenty of times."

"*Why?*"

"They're good for hitting trees and knocking tin cans off fence posts," Clara Jean said matter-of-factly. "The best kind are the ones that are still a little bit mushy 'cause they splat when you throw them."

I knocked on *her* head. "Come on, Miss Cow Chip U.S.A. We've got a p-parade to plan."

"You really ought to try throwing cow chips sometime. It's fun!"

"Remind me to n-never shake hands with you."

"Oh, stop."

"*You* st-stop."

And we ride-walked clear into town.

EPILOGUE

So that was how it all began that one scorching July day in 1950. Clara Jean and I never dreamed our idea for a parade would go over as well as it did.

Everyone had so much fun, Wetumka decided to make it an annual festival. And we picked the perfect name for it—Sucker Day—since we'd all been suckered into F. Bam Morrison's scheme. Except for ol' man Swank, of course, who strutted around preening his tail feathers until his dying day.

I never did buy Clara Jean those fancy new shoes. But Mama and I got her a pair from the Salvation Army. Mama insisted we get a sensible, everyday pair. So we settled on pink-and-white saddle oxfords. Later, when Clara Jean painted pink polka dots on the white parts with borrowed fingernail polish, Mama shook her head. But I wasn't surprised.

After we graduated from high school, Clara Jean decided Wetumka was too small for her, so she moved off to Hollywood and became an actress.

At first, all her acting parts were small, like one of the girls walking around in bikinis in *Beach Blanket Baby Dolls.* Now she's moved up to speaking parts. Last movie she was in, she had ten whole lines— that is, before she got eaten. I think it was called *The Glob That Ate Chicago.*

Every time Clara Jean's in a new movie, she sends me and Mama free tickets to the Redskin Theater. I reckon it's her way of saying thanks for looking after her daddy while she's gone.

Mama and Pastor Regan ended up getting married when I was in sixth grade. At first I didn't like it, having him around all the time. But after a while I got used to him, and it didn't even bother me if he sat in Daddy's chair. I never could bring myself to call him Daddy, though. It just didn't feel right.

I kept practicing on my reel-to-reel tape recorder for two whole years. I learned to talk plumb fine, almost as smooth as glass.

As for F. Bam Morrison, we never saw him again. I reckon he's still going around, town to town, promising things he can't deliver. But even so, I'll always be true-blue thankful for that hot summer day he came strolling down the sidewalk, right into my life.

McCordsville Elementary
Media Center

DATE DUE

PERMA-BOUND ®